D0576203

The BRILLIANT Ms. Bangle

Written by
Cara Devins

Illustrated by
K-Fai Steele

Feiwel and Friends
New York

A Feiwel and Friends Book
An imprint of Macmillan Publishing Group, LLC
120 Broadway, New York, NY 10271 • mackids.com

Our books may be purchased in bulk for promotional, educational, or business use.
Please contact your local bookseller or the Macmillan Corporate and
Premium Sales Department at (800) 221-7945 ext. 5442 or by email at
MacmillanSpecialMarkets@macmillan.com.

Library of Congress Cataloging-in-Publication Data is available.

First edition, 2023
Book design by Aram Kim
The artwork for this book was created with watercolor, ink, and pencil.
Feiwel and Friends logo designed by Filomena Tuosto
Printed in China by RR Donnelley Asia Printing Solutions Ltd.,
Dongguan City, Guangdong Province

ISBN 978-1-250-24770-4 (hardcover)
1 3 5 7 9 10 8 6 4 2

For Patrick and Sienna —C.D.

For the students of the Tenderloin Community School —K.S.

It was the very first day of school at Belford Elementary, and the students were SO excited to be back. They jumped rope on the playground, unpacked their pencil cases, and greeted their friends.

"Over the summer I saw SIX seagulls at the beach!" exclaimed Birdie Frisk.

"I rode in a car for a loooong time to visit my aunt Chelsea," Marty bragged. "She has a poodle named Pepper!"

"And I ate hot sauce by accident," admitted Putnam McFarlane. "I didn't like it."

Summer sure was fun! But everyone agreed it was great to get back to school.

Just as the students settled in, however, they were told some alarming news: The school librarian, Ms. Stack, had moved away over the summer.

"THAT CAN'T BE!" yelped Birdie.

"She was my FAVORITE!" moaned Marty.

"Now, now," said Principal Lyle. "We have a new librarian named Ms. Bangle, and I think you are all going to like her!"

"Not me," muttered Putnam McFarlane.

"Clearly you mean 'Not I.'" corrected Principal Lyle. Putnam rolled his eyes. Clearly Principal Lyle did not understand.

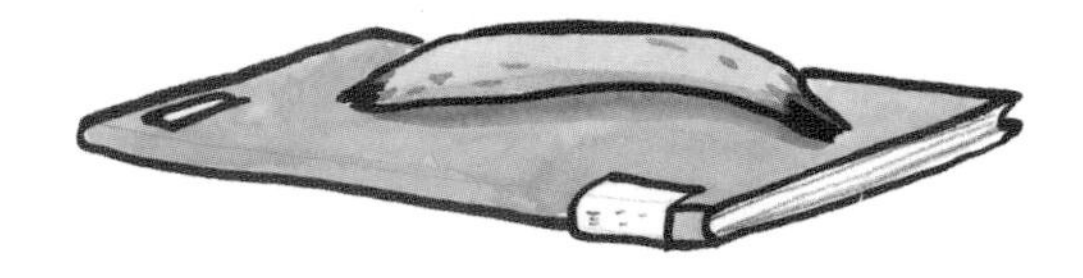

GRAB N' GO
BREAKFAST

The students talked about how much they loved Ms. Stack. She was so nice! She smelled like cinnamon and was always smiling. And last year, she led the students in making bookmarks. Birdie still had hers!

Nope. No one could replace Ms. Stack.

Together the kids hatched a plan:

They would NOT welcome Ms. Bangle. They would refuse, refuse, REFUSE to read with her until Ms. Stack came back.

Everyone loved the plan!

Later, when it came time to go to the library, the students exchanged glances . . .

. . . Then they filed into the library and took their seats.

Where was Ms. Bangle? they wondered. Maybe she'd heard about their plan and simply gone home! That would be lucky!

But all of a sudden, the door swung open. And in walked Ms. Bangle. The students could tell immediately that she was very different from Ms. Stack.

"Good afternoon, children! I'm the new librarian, Ms. Bangle! Here are a few things to know about me: My middle name is Matilda, I've been to Spain three times, and I love peaches. Is there anything you'd like to tell me about you?"

Birdie wanted to tell Ms. Bangle that she loved peaches too . . . but she didn't. Instead she looked down at her shoes.

"Okaaaay. Well, I guess I'll just have to learn as we go! If there's one thing I always say, it's never too late to learn, and you should never have soup before noon. Oops, that's two things!"

BIBLIOT
LIB
圖書

The students had never heard that fact about soup. They really wanted to smile. But they knew better. "So . . . which story should we read today?" asked Ms. Bangle. Nobody answered.

Marty purposely stared out the window and watched the kindergartners playing in the leaves. Ms. Bangle looked around and picked up an old, dusty book.

"How about this one? It's called *The Rise of Lithographic Printing in Eighteenth-Century England*." Marty stifled a giggle.

"Silly me," said Ms. Bangle. "You've probably already read that! What else is there?"

Ms. Bangle picked up a brochure. “How about this? It’s the town parking policies for holidays. Did you know there’s no parking on Celery Street during parades?”

Birdie thought this was hilarious. But she couldn’t let on! In order to stop herself from laughing, she bit down on her lip.

“Ow!” she exclaimed.

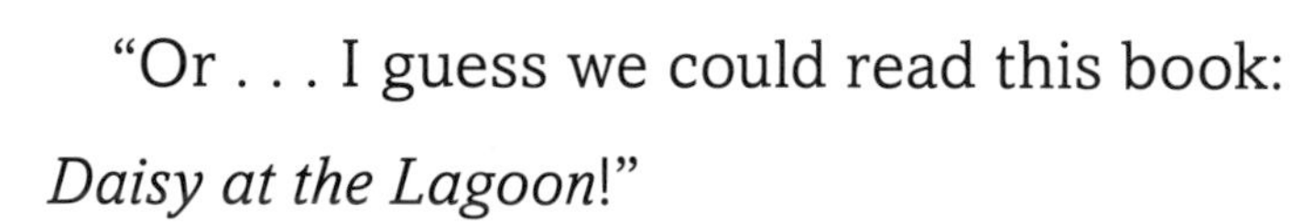

“Or . . . I guess we could read this book: *Daisy at the Lagoon*!”

Ms. Bangle held up a book that looked truly terrific. Putnam had never read it, and desperately wanted to know what was going to happen with Daisy at the lagoon . . . But he knew they couldn’t read it.

DAISY AT THE LAGOON

“We don’t want to read with you!” blurted Putnam. “You’re not Ms. Stack! We love Ms. Stack, and we want her back!”

Ms. Bangle took a deep breath. “Ohhhhh, I see.” She thought for a moment. The students wondered what she would say next. “I wish I could change your minds,” she said, “but I know I cannot.”

“No you can’t!” agreed Birdie.

"I guess this isn't the worst thing," said Ms. Bangle. "I have some odds and ends to take care of . . . a few emails to answer, a pair of pants to hem . . . Oh, and I should call my dear friend Darsha to see how she's recovering from rotator cuff surgery."

What's a rotator cuff? wondered Marty.

"All righty!" said Ms. Bangle, standing up. "I am going to leave you kids over here. But I do need to assign you a few library tasks, since you've given me the afternoon off."

"Of course," said Putnam, wondering what they would be.

"First, I'll need you to sort these and put them all back." Ms. Bangle pointed to a large pile of books. Marty gulped.

"Next I'll need you to take these empty boxes down to the basement. Our new books arrived in them, but now they're just cluttering up the place! If there's one thing I can't stand, it's clutter and burnt popcorn. Oops, that's two things!"

Putnam didn't like burnt popcorn either, but he wasn't about to say so.

"And lastly, Principal Lyle needs your help later to review lesson plans for the fourth and fifth graders. You don't need to finalize them, but you should get close!" Birdie had no idea how to make a lesson plan. She knew how to make toast and say hello in sign language. But neither of those things seemed particularly helpful right now.

"Gracias," said Ms. Bangle. "That's how they say thank you in Spain!" She skipped to her desk and picked up her phone, presumably to call Darsha.

OBJECTIVES
STANDARDS
FRAMEWORK

READ
CIRCUIT STICKERS
BRASIL

"I don't want to go down to the basement, but I don't know how to make a lesson plan!" announced Birdie.

"Okay, I'll make the lesson plans," said Marty. "But I'm NOT going to the basement!"

"Well, why should I go to the basement?" Putnam demanded to know. "I've heard it's dark and smells like lima beans!"

The students were exasperated. They looked over at Ms. Bangle, who they had to admit looked pretty happy.

"All right," said Putnam. "How about we all go to the basement together after we put the books away and do the lesson plans?"

A few minutes into sorting books, however, Birdie began to get bored. This was no fun!

"I think I'd like to read with Ms. Bangle," she whispered.

"Me too!" added Marty quickly.

Putnam hated to admit it, but he agreed.

READ

Together the students approached Ms. Bangle, who jumped when she saw them.

"Oh, hello!" she said. "I forgot you children were even here. Have you had any luck with the lesson plans?"

"Ms. Bangle, we think we might like to read with you after all," said Birdie. "We know you're not Ms. Stack, but you do seem nice . . ."

"And funny!" piped up Putnam.

Ms. Bangle smiled. "Well, okay," she said. "I'll just have to finish hemming these pants later on. If there's one thing I won't stand for, it's pants that don't fit and birthday cakes without candles. Oops, that's two things! I keep doing that!"

The students roared with laughter. They all took their seats in the reading circle and listened intently as Ms. Bangle read *Daisy at the Lagoon*.

Later on, the students began to wonder if pretending she didn't want to read with them had been Ms. Bangle's plan all along . . . If so, they had to admit that her plan was brilliant.

READ

DAISY AND THE HIDDEN ROOM
MAGICIAN
DAISY AND THE PORTAL
DAISY AND THE BIG WAVE
DAISY AND THE OTHER DAISY
DAISY ALONE
DAISY STRANGE ILLNESS
DAISY AND THE TOWER
DAISY AND THE DARK
DAISY AND THE ISLAND